Karen's Pen Pal

**Look for these
and other books about Karen
in the
Baby-sitters Little Sister series:**

Little Sister

Karen's Pen Pal
Ann M. Martin

Illustrations by Susan Tang

A
LITTLE APPLE
PAPERBACK

SCHOLASTIC INC.
New York Toronto London Auckland Sydney

No part of this publication may be reproduced in whole or in part, or stored in a retrieval system, or transmitted in any form or by any means, electronic, mechanical, photocopying, recording, or otherwise, without written permission of the publisher. For information regarding permission, write to Scholastic Inc., 730 Broadway, New York, NY 10003.

ISBN 0-590-44831-5

22 21 20 19 18 17 16 15 14 13   8 9/9 0 1/0

Printed in the U.S.A.   40

First Scholastic printing, February 1992

For Pam Swallow

Karen's Pen Pal

Dear Rocky

*H*um, *de-hum, de-hum.*

I was sitting at my desk in school. I was learning how to write letters. Not the letters in the alphabet. I already know how to write all those letters. I was learning how to write letters that I could send through the mail.

Writing letters is gigundoly fun. (So is getting letters.) My teacher, Ms. Colman, can make almost anything fun. That is one reason I like her.

My name is Karen Brewer. I am seven

years old. I am in Ms. Colman's second-grade class at Stoneybrook Academy. I am the youngest kid in the class. That is because I skipped. The other kids are almost eight. Oh, well. I do not care.

"Listen up, class," said Ms. Colman. "I am going to hand out some paper. Now is your chance to write letters of your own. Each of you may write a letter to someone at home."

I frowned. That was a problem. Should I write to someone in my family in the big house? Or should I write to someone in my family in the little house? Maybe I should write two letters. No. I did not think I would have time to do that.

I gazed around our classroom. Next to me sat Ricky Torres. Ricky is my make-believe husband. We got married on the playground one day. Ricky wears glasses and so do I. So does Natalie Springer, who sits on the other side of Ricky. So does Ms. Colman. Ms. Colman says glasses-wearers have to sit in the front row so they can see

2

better. I think that is a good rule. Except for one thing. My two best friends do not wear glasses. They get to sit together in the back row. My best friends are Nancy Dawes and Hannie Papadakis. We call ourselves the Three Musketeers.

I smiled at Nancy and Hannie.

Then I looked at Pamela Harding. Pamela is my best enemy. She does not like me (much) and I do not like her (much). Pamela's friends are Jannie and Leslie. Pamela and Jannie and Leslie think they are so great. They think they are cool.

These are two more of the boys in my class: Hank Reubens and Bobby Gianelli. Bobby is Ricky's best friend.

We have a pet in our room. He lives in a cage. Our pet's name is Hootie. Guess what Hootie is. A guinea pig!

"Karen, have you started writing your letter?" Ms. Colman asked me.

I stared at the blank paper in front of me. "Not yet," I replied. "I'm sorry." I wrote my address at the top of the page. Now.

Who should I send my letter to? I still could not decide. I did not want to hurt anyone's feelings. But if I wrote to Daddy or someone at the big house, then Mommy and my little-house family might feel bad. And if I wrote to someone at the little house, then my big-house family might feel bad. I sighed.

I looked at Ricky. He was writing busily.

I wrote *Dear* on my paper. Then I had to stop and think some more. Finally I had an idea. I raised my hand. "Ms. Colman," I said, "do we have to write to a *person?*"

"I guess not," replied my teacher.

Goody! Then I would write to Rocky. Rocky is a cat. He lives at the little house. No one would care if I wrote to a cat. Not even Boo-Boo, who is the cat at the big house.

Rocky and Boo-Boo

I bet no one else in my class had trouble deciding where to send his letter. That is because no one else in my class has two homes. But I do. Two homes and two families.

A long time ago my mommy and daddy were married. Then they got divorced. They loved me, and they loved my little brother, Andrew. But they decided that they did not love each other anymore. And they did not want to live together. So

Mommy moved out of our big house. (It is the house Daddy grew up in.) She moved to a little house. Andrew and I moved with her. Both of the houses are here in Stoneybrook, Connecticut.

After awhile, Mommy and Daddy got married again. But not to each other. Mommy married a man named Seth. He is my stepfather. He moved into the little house with us. And he brought along his cat and his dog. His cat is Rocky. His dog is Midgie. I like them very much. But not as much as my rat, Emily Junior.

Daddy married a woman named Elizabeth. She is my stepmother. Elizabeth moved to Daddy's big house. Guess who went with her. Her four kids. Elizabeth has three boys and a girl. They are my stepbrothers and stepsister. The boys are Sam, Charlie, and David Michael. Sam and Charlie are in high school. David Michael is seven, like me, but he goes to a different school. My stepsister is Kristy. She is thirteen. I just love Kristy. She reads to me and plays with me. She is a very good babysitter.

The big house is always busy and full of people. That is one reason I am glad Andrew and I live there every other weekend. (The rest of the time we live at the little house with Mommy and Seth.) Two other people and some pets also live at Daddy's. The people are Emily Michelle and Nannie. Emily is my adopted sister. She is two and a half. Daddy and Elizabeth adopted her from a country called Vietnam. Vietnam is gigundoly far away. I like Emily, which is why I named my rat after her. Nannie is Elizabeth's mother. That means she is my stepgrandmother. Nannie helps with the cooking and with taking care of her grandchildren, especially Emily Michelle. This is helpful because Daddy and Elizabeth both work. The pets at the big house are: Shannon (David Michael's puppy), Boo-Boo (Daddy's grumpy old cat), and Goldfishie and Crystal Light the Second. They are Andrew's and my goldfish.

I have a special nickname for my brother and me. I call us Andrew Two-Two and Karen Two-Two. (I thought up those names after Ms. Colman read a book to my class. The book was called *Jacob Two-Two Meets the Hooded Fang*.) Andrew and I are two-twos because we have . . . two mommies, two daddies, two houses, two dogs, two cats, and two of lots of other things. Andrew and I have a bike at each house. (Andrew's bike is really a trike.) I have two stuffed cats, Goosie at the little house and Moosie at the big house. We have clothes and toys and books at each house. I even have a best friend at each house. Hannie lives across the street and one house down from Daddy. Nancy lives next door to Mommy.

I think being a two-two is lucky and fun. Except for when it isn't. Like when I can only write one letter. And I have to decide where to send the letter, and I hope I am not hurting anyone's feelings.

Dear Rocky, I wrote. (I was glad I had solved my problem.) *How are you? How is the family? I am fine, thank you.*

I wrote the rest of the letter quickly. Then I signed it *Love, Karen.*

Maxie

It was Friday. The kids in my class were a little bit noisy. We are usually a little bit noisy on Friday. That is because we are excited about Saturday and Sunday. (I get noisy on Sundays, too. That is because I am excited about Monday. I love every single day of the week.)

"Class, please settle down!" called Ms. Colman. "You are using your outdoor voices. I would like you to find your indoor voices."

My friends and I stopped talking. We

paid attention to our teacher. This was a good thing, because Ms. Colman said one of my favorite things.

"Boys and girls, I have an announcement."

Yes! One of Ms. Colman's Surprising Announcements! They are usually gigundoly special. I held my breath.

"A friend of mine," said Ms. Colman, "is a teacher, too. Her name is Miss Mandel. She teaches second grade, just like I do. And she has seventeen students, just like I do. But she teaches at a school in the middle of New York City."

"Cool!" I exclaimed. I think New York City is very wonderful.

"The other day," Ms. Colman went on, "I was talking to Miss Mandel on the telephone. I was telling her that you are learning to write letters. Guess what. She said *her* students are learning to write letters, too. I thought that you and Miss Mandel's students could practice writing letters to each other. You could be pen pals."

"Oh, yea!" I cried. I jumped out of my chair. I could not help myself.

Sometimes life is just too exciting.

"Karen, please sit down," said Ms. Colman quietly.

I sat down. But I was still excited. I write letters to lots of people, but I had never written to a real live pen pal. (A real live pen pal is someone you have not met.) I wanted to make a new friend.

Ms. Colman picked up a shoe box. It had been sitting on her desk. "In this box," said my teacher, "are seventeen slips of paper. On each one is written the name of one of Miss Mandel's students. You will draw a piece of paper to find out the name of your pen pal."

Goody! I thought.

Ms. Colman walked around the room. She let each one of us pull a name from the box. When my turn came, I squinched my eyes shut. I reached into the box. I felt around. I chose a piece of paper. Then I opened my eyes and unfolded the paper.

On it was written: Maxie Medvin.

Hmm. Was that a boy's name or a girl's name? I did not know anyone named Maxie. I knew a Max, though. (He was a boy.)

"Class," said Ms. Colman, "each of you may now write a letter to your new pen pal. When you are finished, I will send the letters to Miss Mandel."

I wrote to Maxie with a purple pencil. *Dear Maxie,* I began. *Hi! My name is Karen Brewer. I have two families!* I wanted to write an extra-special first letter to Maxie. So I wrote about my families. Then I told Maxie about all of my pets. Then I said that I had taken some trips. The best one was to Disney World. I also said that I had flown in an airplane by myself — twice. I hoped I had told Maxie about enough good things. I wanted to be a fun pen pal.

When I finished my letter, I wrote *Sincerely, Karen.* Then I wrote, *P.S. Are you a girl or a boy?* I made a paper bookmark for Maxie and slipped it in the letter.

The 50-Yard Dash

I like gym class. It is not my favorite part of school, but it is okay. Some gym things are fun. Fitness Events are fun.

When my gym teacher first told us that we were going to have Fitness Events, I did not know what she was talking about. (My gym teacher is Mrs. Mackey. Her husband is Mr. Mackey, my art teacher!) Then she explained. Fitness Events are ways to test yourself. You can find out how fit your body is. You time yourself to see how fast you can run and how many sit-ups and chin-ups you can do. You keep track of your scores.

I can do ten push-ups really fast, I had written to Maxie.

I was sorry when Mrs. Mackey said we were finished with Fitness Events.

"Maybe we are finished in school," I said to Nancy. "But we can still do Fitness Events at home. We can even make up some new events."

It was the Monday after we had written to our new pen pals. Nancy and I were riding home from school in Mommy's car.

"We could hold our own Olympics!" cried Nancy.

"Yeah! Let's call Hannie when we get home. Maybe she could come over. We could have the Three Musketeers Olympics."

Mommy glanced at us in the mirror. "Girls, it is much too cold to play outside today," she said. "The Olympics will have to wait."

"Aww . . ." I complained.

But Nancy said, "Wait! We could have the Olympics in my basement. My tumbling mats are on the floor, and there's room to run around."

"Yes!" I cried.

Our mothers said we could have the Olympics in Nancy's basement. They let us invite Hannie over, too. Soon the Three Musketeers were sitting on a tumbling mat.

"All right," I said, "I will be the president of the Olympics."

"Wait. How come you always get to be the president?" asked Hannie.

"Yeah. No presidents," said Nancy. "We are three athletes in the Olympics. No one is the president or the head or anything."

"Okay, okay," I agreed. "What will our events be?"

"The ball toss," said Hannie.

"Rope jumping," said Nancy.

"The fifty-yard dash," I said. In that event you have to see how many seconds it takes to run (or dash) 50 yards. I am very good at it. I am a fast runner. (Sorry to brag, but I am.)

Nancy found a pencil and a pad of paper. "I will keep score," she said.

"Okay," said Hannie.

"Hey! Wait a minute. How come you let Nancy keep score, but you will not let me be the president of the Olympics?" I asked Hannie.

We almost had a fight. Then Nancy said, "How about this? We will each score our own events. That is fair."

So we began our Olympics. The first event was the ball toss. Nancy won. She threw a rubber ball so far that it got lost behind the dryer.

Then Hannie won at rope jumping. She jumped 37 times before she missed. (Nancy jumped 31 times and I jumped 24 times.)

I better win the 50-yard dash, I told myself. I had not won anything yet. And I did win, even though we were not sure how

18

far 50 yards was, so instead we ran two circles around the basement.

"A three-way tie!" exclaimed Hannie.

"Yup," I said. That would be something to tell Maxie.

A Letter From Maxie

"Bobby," called Ms. Colman. She handed him an envelope. "Natalie." Ms. Colman handed her an envelope, too.

I sat at my desk. I sat quietly, even though my stomach was jumping around. Ms. Colman was handing out letters from our pen pals! Miss Mandel had sent them to her. I was waiting to hear my teacher call out, "Karen!" Then she would give me a letter from Maxie.

"Karen!" said Ms. Colman.

"Yes! Yes!" I reached for the envelope

Ms. Colman held out. It looked quite fat. I wondered what was in it besides a letter.

I looked at the envelope. Maxie had decorated it. It was covered with stickers. Also rubber-stamp pictures. On the front was written

D –LIVER
  –LETTER
  –SOONER
  –BETTER

D – LATER
  – LETTER
  – MADDER
    I GETTER !

Across the flap of the envelope was written: SWAK. I knew what that meant. Sealed with a kiss!

I tore open the envelope and pulled out Maxie's letter.

Dear Karen,

Hi, it's me. Maxie Medvin. I am a girl. My real name is Maxine Louisa Medvin. I have red hair.

We are going to be great pen pals. We have

21

a lot in common. I do not have two families. But I have twin sisters who are thirteen like Kristy and I have two brothers. They are adopted. We adopted them from South America. Benjie is two and Doug is four months.

I have also been to Disney World. Plus Disneyland — twice!

I collect erasers. My eraser collection is the biggest in my class. I have two hot-air balloons and a dog with rolly eyes and some flowers that smell like flowers and a rainbow and a lot of others. I am sending you two of the smelly flower erasers. Now you can start your own collection. Flower erasers are cool.

I am eight years old. I just had my birthday. How old are you?

I LOVE to read. Miss Mandel says I am the best reader in the whole second grade. I can read FAST.

Please WBS. That means write back soon.
Love, Maxie

P.S. Thanks for the bookmark.
P.P.S. What do you look like?

Well, for heaven's sake. *Twin* thirteen-year-old sisters. *Two* adopted brothers. Disney World *and* Disneyland. *Plus* smelly erasers. And Maxie was *eight*.

"Class?" said Ms. Colman.

I looked up from Maxie's letter. I saw that everyone else had been reading their pen pal letters, too. My friends were smiling.

"Class," said Ms. Colman again, "from now on, your homework will be to write to your pen pal once a week. You may write more often if you like. I will collect your letters and send them to Miss Mandel. Her students will write back to you the same way."

Hmm. So I would have to write back to Maxie. What would I say in my next letter? I could tell Maxie about the Three Musketeers and our Olympics. I could send her a school picture so she could see what I look like. And I could tell her about *my* collection.

Shells and Erasers

I decided to write back to Maxie that very night. So at dinner I said to my little-house family, "Tonight I am going to write a letter to my pen pal. It is for homework."

"What is a pen pal?" asked Andrew.

I sighed. It must be hard to be four and not know anything. "A pen pal," I said, "is a friend you write letters to."

"Is Santa Claus my pen pal?" Andrew wanted to know. "I write to him every year at Christmas."

"No. Santa is not your pen pal."

I let Mommy and Seth explain pen pals to Andrew. I went to my room.

I began my next letter to Maxie.

Dear Maxie,

I got your letter. Thank you! Now I know all about you. Thank you for the erasers, too. They are cool. But guess what. I do not collect erasers. I collect seashells. I think you should collect shells, too.

I stood up then and walked to my shell collection. I have pretty many shells. I have put a label by each shell. The label tells the name of the shell. I found some of the shells myself. I bought some of the shells. And Nannie and Kristy and Daddy give me shells sometimes.

The shells have interesting names like Common Egg Cockle and American Pelican's Foot. I looked in the box labeled Mouse-Eared Marsh Snail. I had *three* Mouse-Eared Marsh Snail shells. I decided to send one to Maxie. I chose the smallest

one and sent it by my letter.

Then I looked at my collection again. I just love my shell collection. I also have a Northern Rough Periwinkle and a False Angel Wing. I have a Tulip Shell from Florida. And I have a Swollen Olive Shell that came all the way from the Indian Ocean. With any luck, I will have a Common Atlantic Octopus one day. I put my collection back on the shelf. If Maxie started a shell collection, she would have to work hard to get as many shells as I have.

I remembered that Maxie wanted to know what I look like. I found one of my school pictures. I wrote LOVE, KAREN on the back.

Then I finished writing my letter. I folded it carefully. I stuck the picture inside. I found a box for the shell. I put everything into a big envelope. I sealed the envelope and decorated it with my fuzzy stickers, which are my very best stickers.

(I did not tell Maxie I am only seven years old.)

Maxie to the Max

Dear Karen,

Hi! It's me, Maxie! I got your letter with your picture. I am sending you a picture of me. I do not wear glasses. I wear contact lenses.

I could not believe it. Maxie got to wear *contacts?* I had asked Mommy and Daddy if I could get contacts. They had said, "No. Not until you are fourteen." And Maxie was only eight. She was older than I was. But she was a long way from fourteen.

I shook the envelope from Maxie. Her school picture fell out. I peeked at it. Maxie looked older than eight, I thought. She looked at least ten. And she was wearing very trendy clothes. She was wearing clothes like Pamela Harding's. On her head was a beret. It matched her polka-dot sweater. And guess what. Her ears were pierced! Even Kristy does not have pierced ears, and she is thirteen. Mommy says girls my age should not have pierced ears. But Pamela's are pierced. And so are Jannie's.

And so were Maxie's. Hmphh.

What does Mommy know?

I picked up Maxie's letter again.

Thank you for the shell. I used to collect shells, too. I collected lots and lots of shells. I collected so many I decided I had enough. So I started my eraser collection instead. I like the Mouse-Eared Marsh Snail shell.

Even though I already have one. Mine looks
different from the one you sent. I am sending
you one of my shells to add to your collection.
I hope you do not have it. It is called an
Angulate Nassa.

I did not have an Angulate Nassa. I
needed one.

Maxie probably had six other Angulate
Nassas. I bet she also had a Common Atlantic Octopus. Or three of them.

Your Olympics sound like fun. I like to
run, too. I am very fast. I like most sports.
I play on a Little League team. I am the
pitcher.

Well, bullfrogs. How come Maxie was
better than me at everything? She was a
fast runner *and* she pitched for Little
League. She had a better shell collection
than I did *and* she collected erasers. She was
older than me. She got to have pierced ears
and contact lenses. Her family was more

interesting than mine. (And mine is pretty interesting.) She had been to Disney World *and* Disneyland.

She was Maxie to the Max.

I did not want to write to Maxie again, but I had to. For homework.

Dear Maxie,
Thank you so, so much for the Angulate Nassa.

I did not tell her it was one I actually needed.

I thought for a moment, chewing on the eraser end of my pencil. What could I say to Maxie? Maybe some more about the Three Musketeers. Hmm, if I wrote to Maxie about my two best friends, she would write back about her *five* best friends. Then I thought, How would Maxie know how many best friends I have? How would she know anything about me? She only knows what I tell her. And I can tell her whatever I want to. So I wrote:

How many best friends do you have? I have eight. They are all the other girls in my class. My best, best friends are Nancy Dawes and Hannie Papadakis. We are the Three Musketeers.

Guess what lives in our room at school. Our class pet. His name is Hootie. Hootie is a monkey.

I know I am not supposed to tell fibs. But my fibs were not going to hurt Maxie.

The Big Apple

"**S**eventeen minus nine is . . . um . . ."

It was math time. I was working very hard on my subtraction sheet. I am good at math, but I do not like subtracting nines. Sometimes I have to talk while I work on a nines problem.

"Eleven minus nine is two," I muttered.

Just as I was writing "2," a spitball landed on my paper.

"Ew, gross!" I cried. "Spitball, Ms. Colman!"

Ms. Colman threw it away for me. "Boys

and girls," she said, "it is time to hand in your papers. Then I want to talk about your pen pals."

Yuck, I thought.

Ms. Colman let us put our chairs in a circle in the back of the room. "What are you learning about your new friends in New York?" she asked. "What are you learning about living in the city?"

Jannie raised her hand. "People live in apartment buildings," she said.

"If they want to play outside, they go to a park or a playground," added Hannie. "Mostly they do not have yards. Anyway, Jen doesn't. Jen is my pen pal."

"New York is called the Big Apple," said Bobby.

"The tall, tall buildings are called sky-scrapers," said Ricky.

"When my pen pal looks out her window," Natalie began, "she sees a grocery store and a newspaper stand and another apartment building."

"Do you know what?" said Hank. "My pen pal lives near a museum called the American Museum of Natural History. Every Saturday he goes there to look at the dinosaur bones."

My classmates kept on talking. I did not raise my hand. I had nothing to say about New York. Maxie and I had hardly written about our lives at all. Mostly, Maxie bragged about things. She was a big old bragger.

"I think I would like living in a city," said Nancy. "I think it would be fun. Eli is my pen pal, and he says New York is fun."

"So does my pen pal, Naomi," said Pamela. "I wish I could meet Naomi sometime. I have her picture and her letters, but one day I would like to see her. And to talk to her for real."

"Yeah! Me, too!" exclaimed a whole bunch of kids.

I felt sort of bad. My friends *liked* their pen pals. They knew about their lives. They

knew about New York City. I only knew about Maxie's collections. And she only knew about my eight best friends.

And about Hootie, the class monkey.

We are both braggers, I thought.

Before the bell rang at the end of school that day, Ms. Colman made a Surprising Announcement.

"Very soon," she said, "we are going to hold a sports celebration."

"Will the whole school celebrate sports?" I wanted to know.

Ms. Colman shook her head. "I do not think so. Mrs. Mackey and I have talked. We know how much this class likes the Fitness Events. We thought we would celebrate sports somehow. We have not made many plans yet. But here is how you can get ready for the big day. You can practice the events you enjoy the most or are the best at. When I know more about the celebration, we will talk again. Until then, keep practicing!"

No problem, I thought. The Three Musketeers would hold some more Olympics. I would run and run. I would become the fastest runner in my class. Maybe in the whole second grade.

Karen's Castle

"The Three Musketeers *have* to be ready," I said to Hannie and Nancy.

"Ready for what?" asked Nancy. She reached into her desk. She pulled out her pink-and-blue Atlantic City pencil case.

"Ready for the sports celebration."

School was over. The last bell had rung. My classmates were leaving the room. (Most of them were walking, but a few were running.)

I waited in the back of the room for Hannie and Nancy. They were stacking up their books and putting on their jackets.

"What do you mean?" asked Hannie.

"Well, whatever it is, we want to win it, don't we?"

"I guess," said Hannie.

"I guess," said Nancy.

"So we better stay in shape. We have to go into training. We need to exercise. We need to keep track of our scores so we can try to beat them. And we need to practice, practice, practice, like Ms. Colman said."

"Heavens," said Hannie.

"Goodness," said Nancy.

"We better get to work in your basement," I told Nancy.

So we did.

We dressed in workout clothes. I wore gym shorts and a T-shirt. Nancy wore a dance leotard. Hannie wore leggings and a sweat shirt.

"Ready?" I called. "It is exercise time. Okay. Hands above your heads, hands on your hips, touch the floor, hands on your

hips, start over. One, two, three, four. One, two, three, four."

We did stretches. We ran around the basement. We practiced chinning and doing sit-ups and dashing. Finally we got tired. We fell onto the tumbling mats in a heap. We were out of breath.

"I think we have practiced enough for one day," I said.

"Good," replied Hannie and Nancy. And Hannie added, "I should call my mother. I better go home now."

"Me, too," I said. "Okay, athletes. This is your mission. To practice. I will see you in school tomorrow. Signing off!"

I ran home. I ran straight to my room. Time to start my homework. I dumped out my book bag. And there was a letter from Maxie.

I sighed. Then I opened the envelope.

Dear Karen,
    We have a class pet, too. Our pet is a cat. Her name is Jazzy. (The boys wanted to call

her Stinker, but the girls would not let them.)
Jazzy is a very good cat. She does not even
have a cage. She just walks around our room.
Sometimes she sleeps under my desk.

Have I told you about my dad? He is a
doctor. When he is not busy being a doctor,
he is a musician. He plays in a rock band.
He plays the drums. In some countries he is
a star.

Maxie's class pet was a *cat?* I had never
heard of such a thing. And her father was
a doctor *and* a rock star?

Maxie had beaten me again. A cat wan-
dering around the room was better than a
caged monkey. A doctor and a rock star
were much more interesting jobs than
Daddy's.

My letters to Maxie must be awfully bor-
ing for her.

Dear Maxie (I wrote),
Have I told you about my dad's house? It
is huge. It is a castle. My room is in one of

the turrets. I like to run across our drawbridge. The drawbridge goes over the moat
around our castle.

Here is how big the castle is. It is so big
that I have not even been in every room. Just
the important ones. . . .

Maxie's Movie

Dear Karen,
    You are lucky to live in a castle. I wish I lived in a castle. At least my apartment is very large. It has twenty-two rooms. Thirteen of them are bedrooms. I can sleep in a different bedroom every night, if I want. There is a TV in each one. (A color TV.)

Dear Maxie,
    Did I tell you about the alligators in our moat?

Dear Karen,

Did I tell you I have been in a movie? I played a girl named Whitney. They dyed my hair blonde so I could be Whitney. In one scene, I had to cry. The director did not have to peel onions or anything. I can cry whenever I want. It is just natural for me.

While I was making the movie, I met four famous stars. I got their autographs. Then they asked for my autograph. I earned about a million dollars. Soon I am going to be in another movie.

Dear Maxie,

Did I tell you about the book I wrote? I mean, I did not just write it. It was published. The title of my book is Karen's Castle. *It is the story of my life. Two million copies of the book have been sold. It is in our school library. People ask me for my autograph all the time. I write my name so much my hand gets tired.*

I can run the 50-yard dash in 8½ seconds.

Dear Karen,
   I can run the 50-yard dash in 8 seconds.

Dear Maxie,
   I have been practicing. Now I can run the dash in 7½ seconds.

Dear Karen,
   How many sit-ups can you do in a minute?

Dear Maxie,
   I have visited more than half the states in our country. How many have you visited?

(I did not answer Maxie's question because I have not practiced sit-ups very much. I guessed it was time to start.)

Pen Pal Day

"Give it!" I shouted.

"Over here!" yelled Ricky.

"No, over *here!*" yelled Hank.

"It's mine. Give it!" I cried again.

School had not even started. Already the boys were playing monkey-in-the-middle. They had made me the monkey. They were tossing around my plastic bottle of pretend perfume. They would not give it back.

"Excuse me."

Uh-oh. That was Ms. Colman. She had come into our room, and she had found us playing around. Well, maybe she would get my perfume for me.

She did not have to. As soon as Ricky saw Ms. Colman, he handed me the bottle. I stuffed it into my pocket.

"Let's get started," said Ms. Colman. "Today is going to be busy."

She was not kidding. That day our teacher made two Surprising *Awful* Announcements. This was the first one:

"Boys and girls, I have some good news. Remember when you wished you could meet your pen pals? Well, you are going to get your wish. In a few weeks, Miss Mandel and her class will come to Stoneybrook for a field trip. They will spend the day with us. You can get to know your new friends better. You can show them our school and introduce them to your other friends. We will plan some special activities."

All around me, my classmates were whispering.

"Awesome!" said Ricky.

"I cannot wait!" said Natalie.

And Pamela Harding jumped to her feet and cried, "Oh, *thank* you, Ms. Colman. You are the best teacher ever!"

I stared down at my hands. This was not wonderful. It was awful. It was a nightmare. I could not believe that Maxine Louisa Medvin would be spending a day at my school. With *me*. Yikes. I tried to remember the stories and lies I had told Maxie. Let's see. I said Hootie was our class monkey. I said I had eight best friends. I said I lived part-time in a castle, and I told Maxie all about the castle. I said I had written a book. I said I had visited more than half the states in our country.

Uh-oh. When Maxie came to my school, she would look for our monkey. She would want to meet my eight best friends. And if she asked anyone about my castle or my book, she would find out that I had lied. (I was probably safe on the story about visiting the states, though.)

"Oh, Ms. Colman, Ms. Colman!" Pamela

Harding waved her hand wildly. "What special activities will we do on Pen Pal Day?"

"We will plan most of the activities together," Ms. Colman answered. "But Miss Mandel and I have already discussed the main activity. We will celebrate sports together. Our Sports Celebration will be on Pen Pal Day. You will compete against your pen pals in the events for which you have been training. Your pen pals will be training for those events, too."

Oh, *no*. Pen Pal Day was growing worse and worse. I had told Maxie I could run the 50-yard dash in 7½ seconds. This was not true at all. The 50-yard dash was my best event, but I was not *that* good. Maxie was probably terrific at every event. She could run the 50-yard dash in 8 seconds. She was the pitcher on her Little League team. I had a feeling she could do about a million sit-ups in a minute.

I hung my head.

I was in Gigundo Trouble.

Meanie Maxie

Dear Maxie,
  Hi. How are you? I am fine. So is my family. I guess you heard about Pen Pal Day. Are you going to come to Stoneybrook?

I had thought of something wonderful. Maybe Maxie would not be able to come on Miss Mandel's field trip. Maybe she would be starring in another movie that day. Or maybe her rock-star father would have to fly to Europe, and he would take his family along.

Dear Karen,

Hi. How are you? I am fine. So is my family. Yes, I heard about Pen Pal Day and I am coming to Stoneybrook. I am excited about meeting Hootie.

Dear Maxie,

Hi. How are you? I am fine. So is my family. Except for my father. He says we might have to sell the castle. Feeding the alligators is expensive. By the time you get here, I might be living in a regular old house. (Well, in two regular old houses.) So if my friends do not talk about the castle, you will know why. They are very sad about it.

Dear Karen,

Hi. How are you? I am fine. So is my family. Except for my father. He might have to give up being a rock star. He is a little old to be a rock star and a doctor. So if my friends do not talk about my father's glamorous job, you will know why. They are heartbroken. They are so sad that they gave away all the tapes and CDs he recorded.

Hmm. Maxie did not seem to mind about the castle. Maybe I could make up a reason why there was no monkey in our classroom. But how could I explain that we had a *guinea pig* with the same name as our monkey? I could not think of a good story. Even if I could have, Maxie might ask Ms. Colman or Hannie or Nancy about our monkey on Pen Pal Day. Maybe if I did not mention the monkey, Maxie would forget about him.

Dear Maxie,
  Have I told you about my pets? I have a rat named Emily Junior and a goldfish named Crystal Light the Second. Also, my families have two cats and two dogs.

Dear Karen,

Even though we live in an apartment, we have lots of pets. We have a tortoise and three hamsters and two guinea pigs and a ferret named Mike and an aquarium full of fish. Plus, there are some snails in the aquarium.

Meanie-mo, meanie-mo, Maxie is a meanie-mo, I sang to myself. Maxie was such a bragger. I would call her Meanie Maxie. I did not know anyone who bragged as much as she did. Every time I said something, Meanie Maxie said something better. Then *I* had to say something better. Maxie had made me a bragger, too. She was the reason I was in Gigundo Trouble.

Still, I had to keep writing to Meanie Maxie. For homework.

Dear Maxie,
   How are you? I am fine.
        Your pen pal,
           Karen

The Winner!

"On your mark, get set, GO!" yelled Nancy.

I ran as fast as I could. I ran straight across the blacktop part of our school playground. I ran so fast I felt as if I were flying.

When I ran past Hannie, she clicked off the stopwatch.

"How fast was I?" I called.

"Eight seconds!" she replied.

Not bad. I had run the 50-yard dash in 8 seconds. That was how fast Meanie Maxie could run 50 yards. And it was faster than Hannie or Nancy could run the dash. I was the fastest Musketeer.

"You're the winner!" Nancy said to me.

My friends and I were practicing for the Sports Celebration. I had decided I would enter the running events. The 50-yard dash was my best event. Maybe I could even beat Maxie.

"One more time!" I cried. "Time me one more time, you guys."

"Aw, Karen, I'm tired of practicing," said Hannie. "Let's do something different. Recess is almost over."

"I'm tired of practicing, too," said Nancy.

Hannie and Nancy trotted over to me. Hannie put the stopwatch in her pocket. Then we linked arms. The Three Musketeers walked slowly around the playground. After awhile we sat on the swings.

"Pen Pal Day is almost here," said Hannie. "I will get to meet Jen."

"And I will get to meet Eli," said Nancy. "Eli lives on the twenty-seventh floor of his apartment building. Can you imagine living so high up? He says when he looks out of his bedroom window he can see the Empire State Building and the tops of the Twin Towers. He can even see New Jersey."

"Cool!" exclaimed Hannie. "Can he see the Statue of Liberty?"

Nancy frowned. "I do not think so. The statue is too little."

"Oh. Jen cannot see it, either, but she has been to it four times," said Hannie. "And last Saturday she ate at a restaurant called Rumpelmayer's. She ate a hot fudge sundae."

"Rumpelmayer's?" said Nancy. She giggled. "Are you sure it wasn't called Rumpelstiltskin's? Like in the fairy tale?"

Hannie laughed, too. "No. Rumpelmayer's. Jen likes the desserts there."

For a few moments, we were quiet. We swung back and forth. Then Hannie said, "Karen, tell us again — what is Maxie's whole name?"

"Maxine Louisa Medvin," I replied.

"Maxine Louisa," Nancy repeated. "That is a beautiful name."

I shrugged. "I guess."

"Did you get a picture of Maxie?" asked Hannie.

" Yup."

"You never showed it to us."

I shrugged again. "It must be at home."

"Eli wears glasses," Nancy commented.

"Jen has braids," said Hannie.

I nodded. I did not feel like talking about Maxie. I had not told my friends that Maxie and I had bragged to each other. I had not told them about my lies — about Hootie or the castle or anything. I was pretty sure Nancy had not lied to Eli, and Hannie had not lied to Jen. I wished I could be excited about Pen Pal Day, like my friends were, but I just was not.

I wished Pen Pal Day were already over.

The bell rang then. "Come on, you guys," I said. "Let's go inside."

"Here They Come!"

I was standing in front of my closet. I had been looking in it for about five minutes. I decided I had *no* cool clothes.

"What am I going to wear today?" I whined.

It was Pen Pal Day. In a few hours I would meet Maxie. I knew she would look very, very trendy and cool. And older.

I wanted to look cool and older, too. (I still had not told Maxie I had just turned seven. What a mess.) How could I look cool, though? I did not own a beret like

Maxie's. I did not have contacts and pierced ears.

Okay, I said to myself. Maybe I cannot look cool. Maybe I cannot look older. But I can get dressed up.

"Mommy!" I called.

Mommy came into my bedroom. "Karen, why aren't you dressed yet?"

"I am still choosing," I answered. "Mommy, today is a special day at school. It is Pen Pal Day. May I wear a party outfit? I want to look nice."

"Okay," said Mommy.

I put on my fancy flowery dress with the big white collar. I put on pink tights and black Mary Jane shoes. I tied a huge pink ribbon in my hair. Then I added some jewelry — a ring from the dentist, and even a pair of clip-on earrings that Mommy had given me for dress-up. I was a Lovely Lady.

That morning I walked proudly into my classroom. The first thing I noticed was that nobody else had gotten dressed up.

Hannie was wearing a jean skirt and a T-shirt.

Nancy was wearing leggings and a long sweat shirt.

Ricky was wearing sweat pants and a turtleneck shirt.

Almost everyone was wearing sneakers. (I had sort of forgotten about our Sports Celebration and the 50-yard dash. I had never tried running the 50-yard dash in my party shoes.)

The second I walked into my classroom, Bobby yelled, "Yo, Karen!"

"Hi," I replied.

"What are you so dressed up for?"

"Yeah," said Hank. "Are you going to a party? Or to a ball?"

"Very funny," I said. I ignored everyone.

Except for Hannie and Nancy.

"I think you look pretty," said Hannie.

"Me, too," said Nancy.

"Thank you." (I was glad they had not asked me how I would run races.)

"Boys and girls, please sit down," said Ms. Colman, just as the bell rang.

We scrambled for our seats.

"Are you ready for your big day?" she asked us.

"Yes!" we cried.

"Are you ready to meet your pen pals?"

"Yes!"

"Are you ready for the Sports Celebration?"

"Yes!"

Pen Pal Day began. Ms. Colman took attendance. She made some announcements (regular ones). She collected homework. She read to us from a book called *Just So Stories*, by Mr. Rudyard Kipling.

Ms. Colman was closing the book when Ricky jumped out of his seat.

"Ricky?" she said. "Please sit down."

But Ricky did not sit down. He was staring out the door and into the hallway. "Excuse me," he said. "I think our pen pals are here. Yup, here they come!"

Hootie and Tootie

I closed my eyes for a few seconds. Maybe this was a bad dream. Maybe when I opened my eyes, no pen pals would be coming down the hall. Maybe I would not even be in school. Maybe —

"Hello, Miss Mandel!" I heard my teacher say.

I opened my eyes. Standing in the doorway was a woman I had never seen before, and a bunch of kids. I knew who they must be.

Oh, bullfrogs.

"Please come in," said Ms. Colman. She turned to my classmates and me. "Boys and girls, I would like you to meet my friend Miss Mandel, and her students, your pen pals."

Our pen pals followed Miss Mandel into the classroom. They stood by Ms. Colman's desk. They looked like any other second-graders, even if they were from New York City. I searched their faces. When I found a redheaded girl, I knew she was Maxie. Maxie was looking back at me. I guess she recognized me, too.

Maxie and I did not smile at each other.

On Pen Pal Day our room was set up differently than usual. At every desk (even Ms. Colman's desk) were *two* chairs. The pen pals were going to stick together all day.

Ms. Colman began calling out names. Soon the pairs of pen pals were sitting together. I was *right next* to Meanie Maxine

Louisa Medvin. She had sat down without saying anything, not even hi. But the other pen pals were talking and laughing.

I decided to take a chance. "I like your shirt," I said to Maxie. My pen pal's shirt was very cool. It sparkled and glittered. Across the front were the words NEW YORK in puffy green writing.

"Thank you," replied Maxie. "I like your, um . . ." (she looked at my outfit) ". . . your class. These girls must be your eight best friends."

"Well, yes . . ."

"Hey, I brought my eraser collection," said Maxie. "Want to see?"

"Sure."

Maxie pulled a tin box out of her book bag. She lifted the lid. Inside were dozens of erasers — all colors, all shapes, and all designs. "Here it is," she said.

"Cool!" I exclaimed.

Right away, Maxie began to brag. "It is even better than my shell collection. But you know what? My uncle sent me a new shell. He sent it all the way from Panama. It is a Prince Murex."

Well, who cared about Maxie's old Prince Murex? "I just got a new shell, too," I said. "I got a Common Atlantic Octopus."

(That was a big, fat lie.)

"*I* am going to get a Golden Moon Shell."

"Good. Want to look around my classroom?"

"Okay. Show me Hootie. I want to see the monkey."

Uh-oh.

I led Maxie across the room to Hootie's cage.

"All I see is a dumb guinea pig," said Maxie.

"I know. Hootie is . . . away. That is Tootie, the visiting guinea pig." Maxie did not look very impressed, so I said, "Now I will introduce you to my best friends." I introduced her to Nancy and Hannie.

"How about the others?" asked Maxie.

"Oh, they are all here. There is Pamela and there is Leslie and . . . " I pointed out the other girls in my class.

I was in such a mess. I would not make it through the day. I just knew it. Maxie was going to find out that I was a bragger and a liar.

New Friends

After my classmates and I had shown our pen pals around the room, Ms. Colman and Miss Mandel asked us to take our seats. I sat at my desk. Maxie sat next to me again.

"Well, you have finally met your pen pals," said Ms. Colman. "You have had a chance to talk. Have you learned anything new about each other?"

"Or about how Stoneybrook Academy is different from our school?" asked Miss Mandel. "Or how it is the same?"

Right away, Maxie raised her hand. "I

like Stoneybrook Academy!" she exclaimed. "It is not so different from our school. Except when you look out the windows, you see trees and bushes and grass."

"I like Hootie," said Eli, who was Nancy's pen pal.

I held my breath. I was waiting for Maxie to say, "How did you get to see Hootie? He is away somewhere." But Maxie did not say that. She had raised her hand again. She was waving it around. She was waving it just like Ricky Torres does when he cannot *wait* to say something.

Miss Mandel called on Maxie again. "Yes, Maxie?" she said.

"This is the funnest thing we have ever done!"

She was right. Sort of. I mean, writing to a pen pal and then getting to meet your pen pal should have been tons of fun. Plus Maxie and I really did have a lot in common.

If only she were not such a horrible bragger.

Hannie raised her hand. "Me and Jen both like to read mysteries about the Bobbsey Twins," she said. "We both like to go to the library."

"Could we see the library at Stoneybrook Academy?" asked Jen. "I want to see if it is like ours."

"I think we could peek in the library," Ms. Colman replied.

Hannie and Jen smiled at each other.

I glanced at Maxie. I was going to try smiling at her. Then I remembered about the Prince Murex and the Golden Moon Shell. I looked away.

Other kids were raising their hands.

"I can walk home from our school," said a boy named Oliver.

"My parents drive me," said Ricky. "I live too far away to walk."

"Sometimes during school we play in the street," said Naomi, who was Pamela's pen pal. "They close off the street so no cars can drive on it. Then we have recess on the sidewalks and all over the street."

"Don't you have a playground?" asked Natalie Springer.

"We have a play *yard*, but it is not very big."

I was curious about the play yard. I wondered what was in it. But I did not ask. Probably, Maxie would have answered my question. And she would have said the play yard had 12 jungle gyms and 35 swings and even a merry-go-round. The kind with horses.

"Where do you play baseball?" wondered Hank.

Oliver raised his hand. "In the park," he answered. "We play stickball in the street and basketball in the yard, but we go to the park for baseball."

"Oh," said Hank. "We can play baseball right on our playground. I have never heard of stickball."

"Stickball is very wonderful," said Maxie. "But I wish we had a playground like yours. That would be so cool!"

I wished Maxie and I had not bragged to

each other so much. I thought maybe we could have been good friends.

My classmates and our pen pals talked about New York City and Stoneybrook and our schools some more. When we were finished, Ms. Colman said, "Guess what, boys and girls. It is time to get ready for the Sports Celebration."

The Sports Celebration

We walked to the gym with our pen pals, two by two by two. The kids who had not worn sneakers were carrying them. We were going to change our shoes in the gym. I walked beside Maxie. She was wearing very cool pump-up running shoes. I was carrying my tired old sneakers. I had found them in my cubby. They were not my best sneakers. But they were better than my party shoes for running around the gym.

In the gym we sat on the floor. We changed our shoes if we needed to. Then

Ms. Colman said, "Boys and girls, please divide into two teams. Miss Mandel's students, come over here and tie these red belts around your waists. My students, tie on these blue belts."

Miss Mandel and Ms. Colman handed out the belts. They looked like karate belts. I tied my blue belt around my party dress. It did not match the pink at all. Then again, the sneakers did not match, either. They were plaid. (And they had holes at the toes.)

"Okay," said Ms. Colman, when the teams were ready, "there will be nine events in our Sports Celebration — three running events, sit-ups, chin-ups, rope climbing, an obstacle course, jumping jacks, and the broad jump. Each of you has signed up for three events. Whichever team wins the most events will be the champions of the Sports Celebration. Is everybody ready to run fast and jump far?"

"Yes!" we yelled.

"The first event will be the broad jump,"

Ms. Colman went on. "Broad jumpers, stand next to me, please."

A bunch of kids ran to Ms. Colman. But not me, and not Maxie.

Maxie and I stood around and watched the broad jumpers.

"What are your events?" Maxie asked me.

"All the running events," I told her. "What about yours?"

"The same. All the running events."

Uh-oh.

My team beat Maxie's team in the broad jump. The next event was the 50-yard dash. Maxie got to be the first runner. She dashed the 50 yards in eight and a *half* seconds.

Humph. Maxie had said she could dash in eight seconds.

When my turn came, I ran as fast as I could. I ran so fast I could feel wind against my face. When I crossed the finish line, my plaid sneakers were flying. I almost ran into the wall.

"Seven and a half seconds!" cried Miss Mandel. "The fastest runner yet!"

When everyone had finished dashing, Miss Mandel's team was the winner. Still *I* had beaten *Maxie*. I felt proud of myself. But Maxie was not happy.

Later, I lined up for the 100-yard dash. So far, we had finished four events. The red team and the blue team were tied two to two.

"Karen! Your turn!" called Ms. Colman.

I set my toe at the starting mark.

Ms. Colman shouted, "GO!"

I ran and ran, but I could not feel the wind against my face. I must have been tired. I crossed the finish line.

"Nineteen seconds!" announced Miss Mandel.

Oh, yuck. My worst time ever.

Then Maxie dashed across the gym.

"Eighteen and a half seconds!" announced Miss Mandel.

Meanie Maxie had beaten me again.

The Tie

"Boys and girls, it is time for our last event," said Ms. Colman.

I drew in a deep breath. My stomach felt nervous. The red team and the blue team were still tied. Now we were tied four to four. The last event was a relay race. Maxie and I were both going to run in it.

The teams lined up, five kids on the red side, five kids on the blue side. Maxie was the last runner on her team. I was the last runner on my team.

Here is what the runners had to do: dash

across the gym, run around a chair, dash back to our team.

The first two runners tied. The second two runners tied. So did the third and fourth pairs of runners.

Now it was time for Maxie and me to run. If I ran faster, I would win the relay race and my class would be the champions in the Sports Celebration. If Maxie ran faster, she would win the relay race and Miss Mandel's class would be the champions in the Sports Celebration. You know what? I did not care too much whether my team became the champs.

I just wanted to beat Maxie.

I think Maxie wanted to beat me, too. She kept glancing at me. Since Maxie and I are so much alike, I knew how she felt.

Maxie and I raced across the gym. *Whoosh!* We ran around those chairs. We ran back to our teams. I ran extra hard. But . . .

"Tie!" announced Miss Mandel.

"Do over!" I called right away. "Maxie and I race again!"

"Yeah!" cried Maxie.

We did not wait for permission. We took off and ran again.

We tied again.

This time Maxie yelled, "Do over!" and I yelled, "Yeah!"

We ran a third time. And we tied *again.*

Maxie and I both yelled, "Do over!"

We were tearing around those chairs when I realized something. We were running too fast. We were out of control.

BLAM! We crashed into each other. We fell down.

The gym became very quiet. Nobody made a sound. Then everyone ran toward us. Somebody called, "Are you all right?"

I looked over at Maxie. She was looking over at me. We smiled at each other. And I realized something else. Maxie had never been in any movie. Just like I had never lived in any castle and had never written any book. Maxie's father had never been a rock star, and her class pet probably was not a cat.

I began to giggle and so did Maxie.

When Ms. Colman reached us, she saw that we were laughing. "I guess you two are okay," she said. "But why don't you sit down for awhile? I think you need to rest. While you rest, your teammates will run the relay race over again."

"Come on, Maxie," I said to my pen pal. I led her to the side of the gym. We sat on the floor and leaned against the wall.

"I'm sorry I lied to you," said Maxie.

"I'm sorry I lied to you, too."

"I just wanted to be your friend. I wanted to be someone you would like."

"Same here."

Maxie and I sat together. We watched the relay race.

Miss Mandel's team won. They were the champions of the Sports Celebration.

I did not care. I was just glad that Maxie was not a meanie after all.

Karen's Pen Pal

When we had finished celebrating sports, it was time to show our pen pals around the cafeteria. We were going to eat lunch together.

Maxie and I walked into the cafeteria with our classes. We held hands so everybody would know we were pen pals.

"Do you have a cafeteria like this at your school?" I asked.

Maxie nodded. "Pretty much. I do not think it is this big, though."

"Well," I said, "you can bring your lunch or you can buy it."

"What do you usually do?"

"Buy it," I replied. "Unless it is too gross. Today the lunch is tunafish platter. That means tuna salad and carrot sticks and a hard-boiled egg."

Maxie and I each bought a platter. Then we sat with our friends. But mostly we talked to each other.

"I guess your father was never a rock star, was he, Maxie?"

"No."

"Is he a doctor?"

"Oh, yes."

"A real doctor?"

"Yup. He is a baby doctor. He delivers babies."

"Cool," I said. "Well, I guess you know I never lived in a castle."

"Yes, but that is okay."

"My father's house is very big, though. It is a mansion. But it is not a castle."

"Your father's house is really a mansion?"

"Yup," I said. "And Mommy's house is small. That is why I call my houses the big house and the little house. Mostly I live in the little house."

"Oh. Our apartment is big. But it is not as big as I said. And it is not big enough for all those pets I wrote to you about. We have one tank of fish. That is all."

"Maxie? I told another lie. We do not have a class monkey. We — "

"I know," said Maxie. "I figured it out. Tootie is really Hootie. And Hootie is the guinea pig. *He* is your class pet." (I nodded.) "I — I also told another lie," Maxie went on.

"About your class cat?" I asked.

"Yes. We do not have a cat in our class. A cat came to visit one day, but then he went home. We do not have a pet in our room. We have plants."

"Plants are nice," I said. "I do not care

whether you have a pet. . . . Hey, Maxie, do you like to roller-skate?"

"Are you kidding? I *love* to roller-skate! I skate in the park. I am not very good, but I have fun."

"I like to skate, too! And I guess I am not very good, either. Once I fell and broke my wrist."

"Yikes. I have never broken a bone," said Maxie.

After lunch, Maxie and I went to the playground. We rode on the seesaw and we talked. Maxie had some ideas for more collections. I told Maxie that I like to play detective sometimes. Maxie said she would try that when she got home.

"You know what?" I whispered to Maxie. "I still have my baby blanket."

"Me, too," Maxie whispered back.

"Also, I am only seven."

"I don't care."

Soon recess was over. Then school was over. Miss Mandel and her class had to leave. Maxie and I had to say good-bye.

90

We hugged. We both said, "I will miss you!" Then we both said, "I promise I will keep writing. Good-bye!"

"Hey, Maxie!" I called. "I don't really dress this way!"

"I know you don't. See you, Karen!"

My pen pal went back to New York.

Dear Maxie, Love Karen

Dear Maxie,

I am so glad you came to visit. I had lots of fun. Guess what. I found a bruise on my leg. I think it is from when we ran into each other in the gym. The bruise is shaped like a turtle. (Honest.) Did you get any bruises?

I am still working on my shell collection. I might start a stationery collection next. I really like the erasers you sent, but I am not sure about collecting them. I hope you do not mind.

Today we let Hootie out of his cage and he ran under Ms. Colman's desk. I thought he would never come out!

Love, Karen

Dear Karen,

I got a bruise, too, but it is very little. It does not look like anything except a bruise.

I do not mind if you collect stationery instead of erasers. A stationery collection is a good idea. I might start one, too. Then we could trade stationery. If I do not start a stationery collection, I think I will start a stamp collection.

That is so funny about Hootie!

Today we had a fire drill. We are supposed to walk to the door. But Eli ran. And guess what. He tripped and fell in a wastebasket!

Love, Maxie

Dear Maxie,

Today I wish I did not have two families. One family is easier. I do not always like being Karen Two-Two.

Love, Karen

Dear Karen Two-Two,

Did you have a bad day? I did. And I do not even have two families. One of my sisters yelled at me. One of my brothers lost my new eraser. I got in a little trouble at school. Yuck.

Love, Maxie One-One

Dear Maxie,

Sometimes I get in trouble, too. Try to remember to use your indoor voice.

I wish I could visit you sometime.

Love, Karen

Dear Karen,

I wish you could visit me, too. Or that I could visit you again. I miss you. But I am glad we write letters.

Love, Maxie

Dear Maxie,

I MISS YOU, TOO!!!

Love, Karen

Dear Karen,

Will you promise me something? Will you promise you will always be my pen pal? Please say yes. (You do not have to.)

Love, Maxie

Dear Maxie,

I promise, promise, promise, I will always be your pen pal.

Love, your pen pal,
Karen

Sorry o Short   Write Back Soon   Sorry o Sloppy

About the Author

ANN M. MARTIN lives in New York City and loves animals, especially cats. She has two cats of her own, Mouse and Rosie.

Other books by Ann M. Martin that you might enjoy are *Stage Fright*; *Me and Katie (the Pest)*; and the books in *The Baby-sitters Club* series.

Ann likes ice cream and *I Love Lucy*. And she has her own little sister, whose name is Jane.

Little Sister

Don't miss #26

KAREN'S DUCKLINGS

Early one Monday morning I stood at the windows in Ms. Colman's room. I was looking into the courtyard. I had found more signs of spring. I saw the tips of some yellow crocus flowers. I saw the tips of some purple crocus flowers and also some white crocus flowers. The green daffodil shoots were growing longer.

Something moved the bushes in one of the gardens. I pressed my face to a window. Maybe I would see another chipmunk.

No. No little striped body ran out. The bushes kept moving.

I kept watching.

A breeze blew aside the branches of the shrubs. And I saw . . . a duck.

"Hey!" I screamed. "There's a duck in the garden!"

Little Sister

by Ann M. Martin
author of The Baby-sitters Club®

More Titles... ➡

The Baby-sitters Little Sister titles continued...

❑	MQ48231-9	#59	Karen's Leprechaun	$2.95
❑	MQ48305-6	#60	Karen's Pony	$2.95
❑	MQ48306-4	#61	Karen's Tattletale	$2.95
❑	MQ48307-2	#62	Karen's New Bike	$2.95
❑	MQ25996-2	#63	Karen's Movie	$2.95
❑	MQ25997-0	#64	Karen's Lemonade Stand	$2.95
❑	MQ25998-9	#65	Karen's Toys	$2.95
❑	MQ26279-3	#66	Karen's Monsters	$2.95
❑	MQ26024-3	#67	Karen's Turkey Day	$2.95
❑	MQ26025-1	#68	Karen's Angel	$2.95
❑	MQ26193-2	#69	Karen's Big Sister	$2.95
❑	MQ26280-7	#70	Karen's Grandad	$2.95
❑	MQ26194-0	#71	Karen's Island Adventure	$2.95
❑	MQ26195-9	#72	Karen's New Puppy	$2.95
❑	MQ26301-3	#73	Karen's Dinosaur	$2.95
❑	MQ26214-9	#74	Karen's Softball Mystery	$2.95
❑	MQ69183-X	#75	Karen's County Fair	$2.95
❑	MQ69184-8	#76	Karen's Magic Garden	$2.95
❑	MQ69185-6	#77	Karen's School Surprise	$2.99
❑	MQ69186-4	#78	Karen's Half Birthday	$2.99
❑	MQ69187-2	#79	Karen's Big Fight	$2.99
❑	MQ69188-0	#80	Karen's Christmas Tree	$2.99
❑	MQ69189-9	#81	Karen's Accident	$2.99
❑	MQ69190-2	#82	Karen's Secret Valentine	$3.50
❑	MQ69191-0	#83	Karen's Bunny	$3.50
❑	MQ69192-9	#84	Karen's Big Job	$3.50
❑	MQ69193-7	#85	Karen's Treasure	$3.50
❑	MQ69194-5	#86	Karen's Telephone Trouble	$3.50
❑	MQ06585-8	#87	Karen's Pony Camp	$3.50
❑	MQ06586-6	#88	Karen's Puppet Show	$3.50
❑	MQ06587-4	#89	Karen's Unicorn	$3.50
❑	MQ06588-2	#90	Karen's Haunted House	$3.50
❑	MQ55407-7		BSLS Jump Rope Pack	$5.99
❑	MQ73914-X		BSLS Playground Games Pack	$5.99
❑	MQ89735-7		BSLS Photo Scrapbook Book and Camera Pack	$9.99
❑	MQ47677-7		BSLS School Scrapbook	$2.95
❑	MQ43647-3		Karen's Wish Super Special #1	$3.25
❑	MQ44834-X		Karen's Plane Trip Super Special #2	$3.25
❑	MQ44827-7		Karen's Mystery Super Special #3	$3.25
❑	MQ45644-X		Karen, Hannie, and Nancy	
			The Three Musketeers Super Special #4	$2.95
❑	MQ45649-0		Karen's Baby Super Special #5	$3.50
❑	MQ46911-8		Karen's Campout Super Special #6	$3.25

Available wherever you buy books, or use this order form.

Scholastic Inc., P.O. Box 7502, Jefferson City, MO 65102

Please send me the books I have checked above. I am enclosing $_____
(please add $2.00 to cover shipping and handling). Send check or money order – no
cash or C.O.Ds please.

Name_____ Birthdate_____

Address_____

City_____ State/Zip_____

Please allow four to six weeks for delivery. Offer good in U.S.A. only. Sorry, mail orders are not
available to residents to Canada. Prices subject to change.   BSLS497